THE MAGIC ROUNDABOUT ™

PATHÉ PICTURES PRESENTS IN ASSOCIATION WITH THE UK FILM COUNCIL AND PATHÉ RENN PRICEL FRANCE 2 CINEMA AND CANAL+ A FILMS ACTION/SPZ ENTERTAINMENT/BOLEXBROTHERS PRODUCTION 'THE MAGIC ROUNDABOUT' TOM BAKER JIM BROADBENT JOANNA LUMLEY IAN McKELLEN KYLIE MINOGUE BILL NIGHY ROBBIE WILLIAMS RAY WINSTONE ASSOCIATE PRODUCERS CLAUDE GORSKY LINDA MARKS BRUCE HIGHAM ANDY LEIGHTON VERTIGO PRODUCTIONS BASED UPON ORIGINAL CHARACTERS CREATED BY SERGE DANOT WITH THE PARTICIPATION OF MARTINE DANOT CO WRITERS RAOFF SANOUSSI STÉPHANE SANOUSSI SCREENPLAY BY PAUL BASSETT DAVIES WITH ADDITIONAL MATERIAL BY TAD SAFRAN EXECUTIVE PRODUCERS FRANÇOIS IVERNEL CAMERON McCRACKEN JILL SINCLAIR JAKE EBERTS PRODUCERS LAURENT RODON PASCAL RODON DIRECTED BY JEAN DUVAL FRANK PASSINGHAM DAVE BORTHWICK © PATHÉ FUND LIMITED 2004 ACTION SYNTHESE

First
published in Great
Britain in 2005 by HarperCollins
Children's Books. HarperCollins *Children's
Books* is a division of HarperCollins
Publishers Ltd.

1 3 5 7 9 10 8 6 4 2

0–00–718353–4

THE MAGIC ROUNDABOUT™

The Novel

HarperCollins *Children's Books*

prologue

Everyone stared in horror as the motor-trike sped towards them. From the trike's basket, Dougal waved frantically.

"Look out!" he cried.

They scattered in all directions, and then turned... to see... the motor-trike plough straight into The Magic Roundabout!

The Roundabout shuddered and slowed down, the happy music fading into silence. Sparks leapt from the hole in its roof.

"Whoa!" said Dylan, "bad trip."

The Roundabout ground to a halt.

"It's not good, is it?" whispered Brian.

A great explosion tore through the canopy of The Roundabout.

Basil and Coral screamed. Florence ran to help them. As she climbed aboard, The Roundabout lurched back into motion, turning in the wrong direction.

"It's out of control!" cried Mr Rusty, pulling on the control levers.

Florence took the children by their hands and led them to the central column of The Roundabout.

"Hold on tight, and everything will be fine," she said, trying not to let them hear the fear in her own voice.

As The Roundabout whirled, an incredible thing happened; ice began to form on the roof. It covered the entire canopy, then spread down the sides, blocking any means of escape.

Florence, Mr Rusty and the children were trapped! Another explosion rocked The Roundabout. A figure blasted through the hole in the canopy. It disappeared into the distant, snow-covered mountains. A final explosion tore a toy soldier from the canopy and launched him in the same direction.

The Roundabout stopped. An icy mist billowed out from it, freezing everything it touched.

Dougal ran to The Roundabout and pressed his nose against the ice.

"Florence? Are you all right?"

There was no reply.

A cough from behind made him turn. Looking at him sternly were Dylan, Brian and Ermintrude.

"Dougal," said Ermintrude. "You have some explaining to do."

chapter 1

I only wanted to get my teeth into some sweeties.

Dougal has some explaining to do — let's hear it straight from the dog's mouth.

"I do?" I asked, sheepishly.

"Yes," said Ermintrude. "You can explain just what you think you were doing interrupting my rehearsal (which was going swimmingly, by the way – I was note-perfect as always), how you came into possession of a motor-trike loaded with candy, and why you decided to drive it at full speed into The Roundabout, causing that mayhem!"

She pointed at The Roundabout.

"You noticed, then?" I sighed.

"Oh dear. I had better come clean, I suppose."

"It all happened because I was late. I knew the candy delivery was due at twelve o'clock and I wanted to intercept, er, catch the candy seller before he got to the shop. I dashed across the village as quickly as I could, but when I got to the square, your rehearsal was in full swing and I couldn't avoid it. Er, I mean, I couldn't bear to miss it."

Ermintrude preened herself.

"Yes, it would have been very disappointing if you had missed it," she said. "Disappointing for you."

"Anyway," I carried on. "When you tried to hit that really high note..."

"I did hit it, dear," corrected Ermintrude. "I always hit them."

As if.

I sighed again. "Anyway, I dashed off to meet the Candy Seller."

"I saw you leaving," said Brian. "Why did you grab a drawing pin from one of Ermintrude's concert posters?"

I ignored him. Little troublemaker.

"When I got to the road into town, I was just in time to see the Candy Seller have a nasty accident right in front of me! His trike had a puncture, would you believe?! I offered to stay and look after his trike and its precious, precious cargo while he went to fetch help. He was lucky I was there."

"Hmm," said Brian. "What caused the puncture?"

"It was, um, the drawing pin," I said, blushing. "It just sort of, well, fell onto the road a moment before he arrived. Terrible coincidence. Ahem."

What a bummer!" said Dylan. "That kind of bad luck is just, like, totally unbelievable."

"As you all know, when I say I'll do something, I do it," I said, glaring at Brian, who seemed to be enjoying himself.

"I'd said I would take care of the candy, and I was going to. So, in order to take care of the lovely caramel creams, delicious sherbet lemons and tasty, tasty lollipops, I hopped aboard the trike. My foot must have knocked it into gear, because before I knew it, I was stuck head-first in the basket and headed straight for the village in reverse. You all know what happened next, but it's all right – I'm not too badly hurt."

"Man, what a trip," chuckled Dylan, waving his arms around like an out of control surfer. "You were like, whoa! And then, like, whoooa! again, and then you got thrown out, and like, totally..."

He stopped laughing.

"...crashed into The Roundabout."

We walked around the frozen Roundabout, looking for any signs of life. I peered through the ice. I could just make out Florence's features on the other side.

"Dougal!" she cried. "I'm cold!"

"Don't you worry, Florence," I shouted back. "We'll get you out of there!"

I turned to the others.

"There's only one thing to do at a time like this," I said, grimly.

They nodded. Together, we shouted:

"Zebedee!

Zebedee!

Zebedee!"

chapter 2

I HOPED THIS DAY WOULD NEVER COME

So, can Zebedee help?
Here he is now!

I pride myself on being punctual, so when I get a call for help like that one, I pull out all the stops and get myself there as fast as my spring will carry me.

I knew something was wrong as soon as I saw their crestfallen faces.

"Zebedee! Thank goodness," cried Brian, when I arrived.

"Whatever's the matter, my friends?" I asked.

"Something awful has happened," said Ermintrude, pointing with her tail.

I looked round. When I saw The Roundabout I knew exactly what had happened. My heart sank.

"I hoped this day would never come," I said.

"What, Tuesday?" asked Dougal (he's easily confused). "Tuesdays are great! Tuesdays we bake cakes!"

"No, Dougal, not Tuesday," I said. "The day Zeebad escapes."

They gasped.

"Zeebad? But he's just a shaggy dog story," said Dougal. "Isn't he?"

"I'm afraid not," I said. "He's all too real. Cold-hearted, tyrannous and cruel. And now you've released him..."

I looked at Dougal.

"...He's free to wield his terrifying power once more."

Dougal looked at the ground.

"There are three enchanted diamonds which give Zeebad his power," I carried on. "For thousands of years, he kept our world bound in ice. Many, many years ago, when I defeated and imprisoned him, I hid those diamonds away. Even now, he will be searching for them. If he finds them he will freeze the sun forever. Then nothing will grow, not even grass!"

Dylan woke with a start.

"Okay, people," he said. "We've got a problem."

I continued. "Only by returning the diamonds to their original places on The Roundabout will you defeat him. One of them is hidden here in The Roundabout. I must stay to guard it. To find the other two, you will need this map."

I pulled a crumpled sheet from my tunic, and unfolded it.

"You must head North into the mountains. There is no time to waste. In three days, The Roundabout will be completely frozen and Florence and the children..."

I didn't finish the sentence.

"Well, I hope you've provided us with an appropriate means of transportation," said Ermintrude sniffily.

I produced my magic box and pressed the big red button. A train appeared, as if by magic. Which it was, of course.

"Toot-toot!" said the train.

I handed the magic box to Dylan.

"Take good care of this little box of tricks. It may save you in your hour of need."

Dylan, Brian and Ermintrude boarded the train. Dougal lingered by The Roundabout.

"We're leaving, Florence," he shouted through the ice. "Don't worry – we'll get you out of there!"

We could barely hear Florence's reply. "Don't be too long," she said. "And whatever you do, you mustn't blame yourself!"

"No," said Ermintrude. "Leave that to us."

"My feet are cold," moaned Basil, from inside the ice.

"Don't worry," Florence comforted him. "Our friends will save us."

Dougal hopped aboard and the train set off with a happy "toot-toot" – in completely the wrong direction!

I watched as it turned left, then right, then finally zig-zagged off on what was roughly the right course.

I hoped Florence was right.

chapter 3

Here comes mad, bad Zeebad!

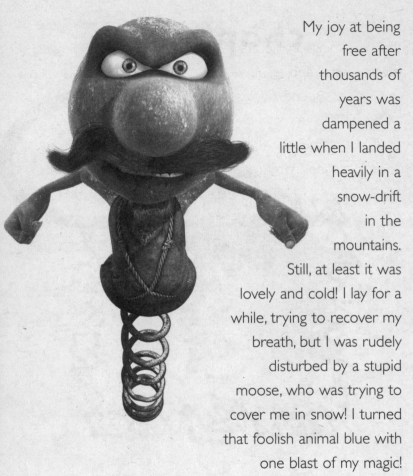

My joy at being free after thousands of years was dampened a little when I landed heavily in a snow-drift in the mountains. Still, at least it was lovely and cold! I lay for a while, trying to recover my breath, but I was rudely disturbed by a stupid moose, who was trying to cover me in snow! I turned that foolish animal blue with one blast of my magic!

With every moment that passed I could feel my powers returning. My moustache crackled with energy. I was back, and I was badder than ever!

"Free at last!" I cried. "It took ten thousand [...] the best things in life are worth waiting for! Like p[...] revenge, and... and, er, power!"

I looked around, drinking in the icy landscape. I shivered with delight.

"Cold," I mused. "But not cold enough for my liking. Soon it will be frozen everywhere, just like it was before Zebedee ruined everything!"

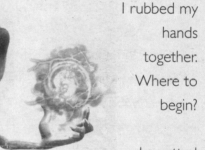

I rubbed my hands together. Where to begin?

I spotted something half-buried in the snow. I picked it up and examined it. It was a toy soldier.

"Just what I need," I cried. "A henchman!"

I tossed him back into the snow, aimed my moustache and zapped him with all the magic I could muster.

He grew to a more useful size, then his eyes opened. He stood to attention and saluted me, his new master.

"Perfect!" I cried. "A lean, mean fighting machine who'll obey my every command! What's your name, soldier?"

"Sergeant Sam, First Decorative Clockwork Regiment, sah!" he replied.

I stared at him sternly.

"Good! From now on your mission is to help me recover three diamonds, stolen from me by a treacherous thief. The road will be hard. Pain, misery and torment will be your constant companions and your only release will be death!"

He was silent for a moment, then:

"Can I ask about holidays?"

"Three weeks in summer," I said.

"Very generous, sir," he replied.

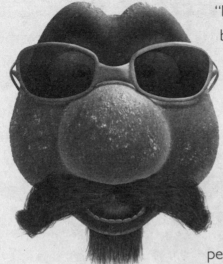

"Not that it will ever be summer again!" I laughed.

I gathered up a handful of snow and pressed it into a ball. One burst from my moustache and the snowball became a crystal. I peered into it.

"Now, let's see what that worm Zebedee is up to."

In the crystal I could see a funny-looking dog, a pink cow, a snail and a dozy rabbit boarding a train.

"Well, well, it looks like Zebedee has some friends to do his dirty work for him these days. I'll soon take care of them!"

I squeezed the crystal until it shattered.

"To my old lair, Sam! We must plan our line of attack!"

chapter 4

WHY DO I HAVE TO BE THE GUARD DOG?

Looks like Zeebad means business! What can Dougal do about it?

It was very quiet on the train when we set off. As we looked back at the village, we could see the ice spreading already.

"Goodness, it's cold," said Ermintrude, shivering.

"Don't feel guilty just because it's all your fault, Dougal," said Brian.

He frowned. "Sorry, that didn't come out right."

"My fault?" I exclaimed. "What did I do?"

Ermintrude turned to me and smiled. "Apart from wrecking The Magic Roundabout, trapping Florence, Mr Rusty and the children in an icy prison, and allowing a maniac to escape and freeze the sun?"

"I only wanted to get my teeth into some sweeties," I sighed. Surely they could understand that?

Dylan raised an eyelid. "It starts with some sweeties, maybe an iced bun, and before you know it you're on two bags of sugar a day. Maybe you've got a problem, my furry friend?"

"I have not!" I retorted. "And I'll not rest until I've done everything in my power to bake things right."

They looked at me.

"Make things right," I said, quietly.

We travelled until darkness fell, then set up camp by the light of the full moon. Dylan and Ermintrude were organising the beds, Brian was cooking, and I was acting in a mostly supervisory role.

"I must say you're all doing a wonderful job," I said, doing my best to boost morale. "Keep up the good work."

Not one of them looked up from their tasks.

"So it's the silent treatment, is it?" I said to myself. "Well, I think I'll just enjoy a little something from my secret supply. Mmmm!"

I went to my tent, where I'd stashed my emergency bag of gobstoppers. I picked them up and sat down beneath an icy overhang to enjoy them.

Ermintrude and Dylan were admiring the landscape.

"What a perfect venue for an open air Verdi festival," she said. "People would flock here."

Obviously inspired by the view to inflict pain on our ears, she opened her mouth and let out a hideous shriek.

La la la la LAAAAAA!

Dylan looked at her with one eyebrow raised.

"Not even sheep would flock to that noise!" he said.

Nothing puts Ermintrude off her singing, however. As she climbed the scale, screeching higher and higher notes, I noticed some icicles above me starting to tremble.

I had no time to move. Ermintrude put a little extra screech into her next note and the icicles snapped! They speared into the ground, skewering my stash of precious gobstoppers. A single, lonely sugary ball rolled intact from the carnage.

"My gobstoppers," I wailed. "There's only one left!"

Ermintrude was oblivious to my tragedy.

"Right!" she said. "It's time we all got some beauty sleep."

"Someone should keep watch," I said, "and I was thinking..."

"Good of you to offer, Dougal," said that slimy Brian, before disappearing inside his shell. "Goodnight!"

"Eh?"

"Goodnight, darlings," said Ermintrude, closing the flaps of her tent behind her..

"But..."

"Night, Ermindude," called Dylan, crawling through his doorway.

"This isn't..."

"Toot-toot!" said the train, and rolled gently into his tent.

I was all alone. I sighed. Deeply.

I patrolled the area for hours, and found myself a little way from the campsite.

"Why do I have to be the guard dog?" I said, to no-one in particular. "What's wrong with a guard snail or guard cow or ..."

There was a shuffling noise behind me.

"Who goes there?" I cried, in my bravest and most commanding voice. "Friend or foe?"

It was a blue moose. How odd.

"Hello, moose," I said. "Feeling a little blue? You're not the only one."

A far less friendly-looking figure appeared, silhouetted against the moon.

"Is... is this a friend of yours?" I asked the moose, hopefully.

The moose bellowed and ran off. I felt bluer than ever.

"I'll take that as a no," I said, trembling.

The figure came closer, cackling horribly.

chapter 5

THIS TORTURE BUSINESS IS ALL A LITTLE NEW TO ME

Left, right, left, right... here he comes — Soldier Sam!

We captured the prisoner with little fuss, then marched him back to Zeebad's secret lair. When we got there, Zeebad used his magic moustache to make a cage of ice for him, which I thought was very clever.

While Zeebad had a little chat with our hairy guest, I put on my apron and got busy with the feather duster. A clean barracks is a happy barracks, you know.

"Now, you dim-witted draught-excluder," said Zeebad to Dougal. "Tell me everything!"

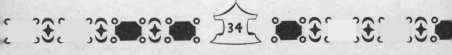

Through chattering teeth, Dougal began: "W–w–well, I was a very happy puppy. My first memories are of catching tennis balls with Florence. Then as I grew up, she..."

Zeebad lost his temper. "NO, you follically-challenged freak! Tell me about the diamonds or I'll make you wish you'd packed a pooper-scooper!"

I had already noticed that Zeebad had quite a temper.

"Me?" said Dougal. "I don't know anything. I don't even have the map!"

"So there's a map?" said Zeebad, smiling.

Dougal looked guilty. "Er, no. There's no map. Sorry. Forget about the map. No map."

Zeebad thrust his face right into Dougal's. He glared at him, eye-to-eye. "Well, of course they'd never trust you with it. You're just a silly little dog. You'd probably just bury it or chew it. So, who does have the map? Eh?"

"I'll never tell!" said Dougal, sounding almost brave, even though his teeth were still chattering.

"Oh no?" grinned Zeebad. "Sam – stop mincing around with that duster. Torture this boarding-house for fleas until he tells us everything!"

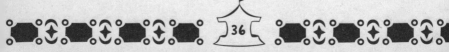

I gave my best salute. "Yes, sir!"

Zeebad sprang over to the mirror to groom his moustache. I untied my apron, and approached the cage nervously.

"Right, then," I said, in my loudest voice. "Torture!"

I leaned closer to the cage so Zeebad wouldn't hear.

"Look, this torture business is all a little new to me," I whispered. "So, er, what is it you're most afraid of?"

Dougal thought for a moment.

"Hmmm," he said. "Sugar, I would say. Horrible stuff."

Well, you never know what strange things people have phobias about, do you? I fetched a nice big bag of sugar lumps from the larder and set about force-feeding them to Dougal, all the while feeling like a downright meanie. Being a soldier can be a dirty job.

Dougal took his torture like a real hero. I fed him sugar lump after sugar lump and still he refused to talk. He was almost grabbing them from my hand, as if to show he would never be broken. I thought he was probably the bravest dog I had ever met.

"Twenty-six..." I counted.

"I can't stand it," moaned Dougal, snatching the next lump from my hand.

"You've eaten twenty-seven sugar lumps!" I exclaimed. "You can't possibly take much more of this! Just tell me!"

A look of defiance came into Dougal's eyes. "You'll have to feed me a hundred before I tell you anything!"

I stuffed another lump into his mouth.

"No, no!" he cried, crunching defiantly on the sugar. "You wouldn't! Would you?"

"How long is this going to take?" I wondered. "I'm working flat out!"

I heard a swishing noise above my head. I looked up to see what was making it. Everything went bright pink, and then horribly black.

chapter 6

WHOEVER HEARD OF A TALKING MOOSE?

What's going on? Let's find out from the udderly brilliant Ermintrude!

When we got up next morning, there was no sign of Dougal. Now we all know that dogs can be very silly, but even Dougal wouldn't wander off in the middle of an important mission.

"Doooooougal?" I cried into the mist (using a high C for distance, if you must know).

"Here, Dougal! Here!" shouted Brian.

"Dooooogie?" yelled Dylan.

"Maybe these will lead us to him," Brian said, pointing to a trail of footprints he'd found in the snow.

Dylan pointed some way ahead. "Or maybe it'll lead us to that."

I looked where he pointed. At the end of the trail stood a blue moose. Yes, blue!

The moose waggled its head and jabbed with its antlers.

"I think he's trying to tell us something," said Brian.

He wriggled his way over to the moose. "Have you seen our friend, Dougal? He's got a black nose, looks like a bad–hair day on legs?"

The moose waggled its head again, faster this time.

"You're wasting your time, Brian," I said. "Whoever heard of a talking moose?!"

The moose jabbed its antlers in the same direction as before.

It was enough to convince Brian. "I think he wants us to follow him. Come on! As fast as you can!"

We followed the moose across the icy wastes until he stopped next to a hole in the ice and cocked his head, as though he was listening. We fell silent and listened too — suddenly, Dougal's voice could be heard as plain as day!

"NOOO!" he cried, pitifully. "It'll take more sugar than that to make me talk, you fiend!"

Brian gasped. "It's Dougal! He's been kidnapped and he's being tortured with sugar to make him talk!"

"Gosh," muttered Dylan. "It could take all night!"

"We must rescue him," I decided.

I cast an eye over the others' flabby physiques and resolved on a plan. "I'm the lightest here. You two can lower me down and I will set him free."

So it was that I found myself being heroically lowered into Zeebad's lair! As I descended, Dougal's moans and groans became clearer and clearer. I looked down. Dougal was locked in an icy cage, being fed sugar lumps by a soldier. I tugged on the rope to give the signal and Brian

and Dylan let me go. My fall was broken nicely by the soldier, who very conveniently went straight to sleep without raising the alarm. I got to my hooves and set about picking the lock of Dougal's cage with my tail.

"You're killing me!" cried Dougal, cleverly keeping up the pretence that he was being tortured.

The lock clicked open. Dougal beckoned me closer.

"Could you come back in five minutes?" he whispered. "I was just beginning to enjoy myself."

The poor dear had obviously gone out of his mind. It is a very small mind, after all.

"What are you talking about?" I hissed back. "It's me, Ermintrude!"

I grabbed him by the collar, and tugged on the rope again. Dylan and Brian started to pull us up.

"Finish him off, Sam," came a voice from the next room. "It's time we..."

Zeebad appeared in the room below us. When he saw Sam asleep on the floor, he dashed over to him.

"The dog!" he cried, slapping Sam to revive him. "What have you done with him, you idiot?"

Sam struggled to speak.
"Ooh! Flattened, sir... flying
pink... cow... from
above..."

Zeebad looked up
and saw us! He sprang into
the air and grabbed my tail.

"Not so fast!" he
cried.

"Ow! Let
go, you
brute!" I
yelled back. My tail
was smarting.

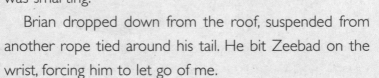

Brian dropped down from the roof, suspended from
another rope tied around his tail. He bit Zeebad on the
wrist, forcing him to let go of me.

"Brian," I cried. "You saved me!"

Dylan pulled us all back to the surface (no mean feat
for one rabbit – Brian and Dougal are not as trim as they
might be). We fled across the ice, until we came across a
hole which led into a tunnel.

"Keep going!" yelled Dougal.

We kept going until the tunnel suddenly became steeper, MUCH steeper, and we found ourselves sliding down, down, down! Brian, taking advantage of his low-drag body shape, surfed his way down with ease while the rest of us bumped and crashed against one another all the way.

Brian suddenly threw himself sideways and ground to a stop. We dug our hooves, paws, claws, teeth and tails into the ice and just managed to stop ourselves flying over a ravine and into a deep, deep crevasse.

"Whoa, man, that is deep!" said Dylan, looking over.

"I think we've reached the end of the line," said Brian.

"You took the words right out of my mouth," said a rather unkind voice, from behind us.

Zeebad and Sam were advancing upon us.

"Sam," said Zeebad. "Your sword!"

"Sir!" cried Sam, pulling his sword from its scabbard.

"No—one can save you now!" cackled Zeebad.

"Hey, man," said Dylan. "Give peace a chance."

I looked at the others. Dougal nodded. We called out:

"Zebedee!

Zebedee!

Zebedee!"

chapter 7

REVENGE IS A DISH BEST SERVED COLD

The gang are cornered! Is this the end? Zeebad thinks so...

We had them trapped! As we drew nearer, I could feel how close I was to getting the map... and my diamonds! Then, of course, the silly fools called for Zebedee. Yawn, yawn, yawn. How very predictable.

Like the sentimental, eager-to-please fool he's always been, Zebedee arrived in a trice.

"Zipadi-dee, zipadi-da!" he sang.

"You!" I thundered.

"So we meet again," he said, cockily.

We faced one another. Somehow, I knew that this time I would win.

"I've waited ten thousand years for my revenge, Zebedee," I hissed. "And as you know, revenge is a dish best served cold."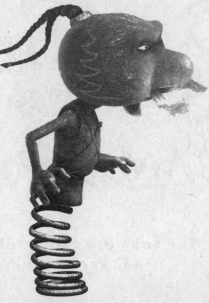

He smirked. "Some like it hot, Zeebad."

My pictures...

This is me before everything went so very, very WRONG! A picture of innocence...

I was only trying
to get my paws
on some sweeties.

But I ended up in BIG trouble. Of course I was extremely brave, even when I was tortured horribly.

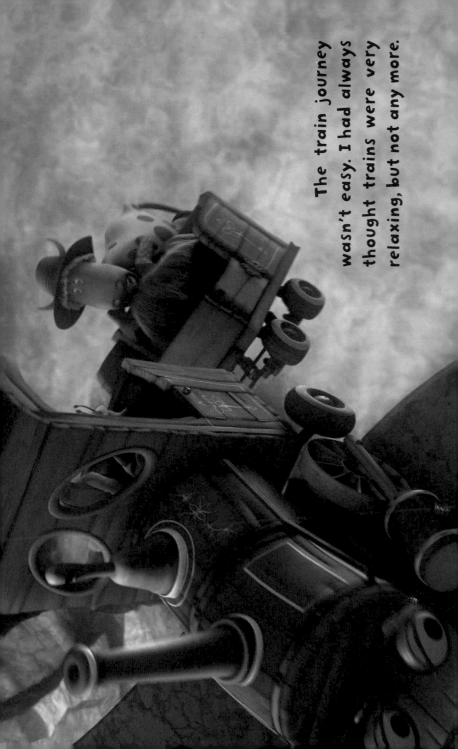

The train journey wasn't easy. I had always thought trains were very relaxing, but not any more.

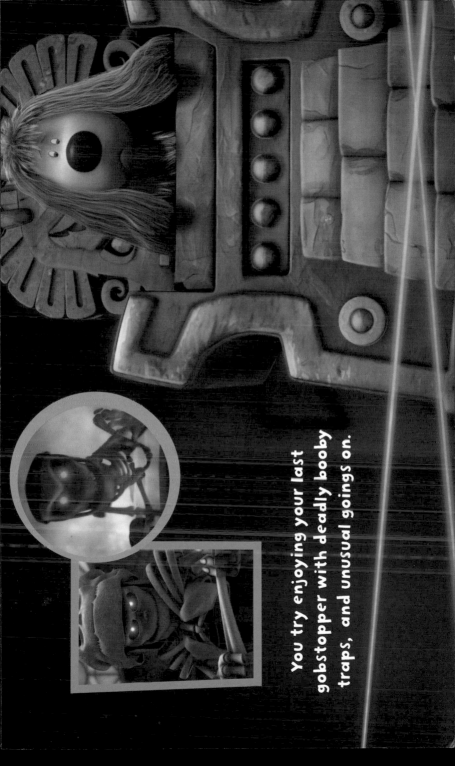

You try enjoying your last gobstopper with deadly booby traps, and unusual goings on.

On more than one
occasion I thought
we were done for.

By the time
we got back to
The Roundabout it
was almost too late!

But every dog has his day!

I powered up my moustache and fired an icy blast at him. He side-stepped and it missed, but only just. I fired another. This time, he sprang into the air, my blast passing harmlessly below. I leapt to meet him and we collided in mid-air. I was forced over the edge of the crevasse, but managed to grab hold of an icy outcrop as I fell.

I caught my breath, then started to pull myself back up. As I hauled myself over the edge, I could see those pesky animals running away. Sam blocked their way, using his sword to stop them in their tracks.

"Oi!" he shouted. "Where do you think you lot are going?"

"Sam!" cried Zebedee. "Stop! Think about what you're doing!"

"It's not my job to think," he shouted back. "I'm a soldier. I'm just following orders."

Good boy, Sam!

"You may wear a soldier's uniform, Sam," said Zebedee, "but it's what's inside that counts."

I was back on solid ice. I took my chance to aim another icy blast at Zebedee's back, but that stupid dog saw me.

"Look out, Zebedee!" he yelped.

I aimed a rapid-fire left-right combination of shots at Zebedee, forcing him closer and closer to the crevasse.

"Run!" he yelled to his friends. "Run!"

The snail slithered back up the tunnel.

"Come on, gang! Now's our chance to escape," he cried.

I aimed a blast right for Zebedee's spring. It was a perfect shot! He was iced to the spot, only inches from the edge.

"Your days in the sun are over, Zebedee, you benevolent bed-spring," I gloated (and there's nothing wrong with a good gloat). "Now it's time for Zeebad!"

I fired a concentrated beam of energy at the ice beneath his spring and started to cut through it.

"Zebedee's in trouble!" howled the dog.

"Save yourselves!" cried Zebedee, waving them away.

"What shall we do? What shall we do?" said the stupid hound, running in circles.

"We can't leave him," said the snail. "To the rescue!"

Back they came, as though they could somehow rescue Zebedee from me!

Zebedee waved furiously at them again.

"You've got to find the diamonds!" he yelled.

I turned and fired at the roof of the tunnel entrance.

A shower of icicles fell, stabbing into the ground point-first. They stuck there, forming a barricade. I didn't have to worry about them any more!

I turned back to my springy enemy. One more blast would do it, I thought. I fired. A crack appeared in the ice. It got bigger, widening until finally the ice split right through. Zebedee, still frozen to the icy outcrop, tumbled into the crevasse.

"Zebedee!" yelled the dog.

I watched as Zebedee tumbled further into the crevasse, a smile upon my face.

"And so it ends," I said. "My nemesis, finally vanquished forever."

"Get the diiiaaaamooooonds!" cried Zebedee, his voice fading as he fell into the darkness.

Sam picked himself up gingerly, and joined me at the edge of the crevasse.

"It's almost enough to make one weep..." I said. "If only I wasn't so very, very happy. Ha ha ha! Now nothing can stand in my way! MWAAHA HA HA HAAAA!!!"

"Hyik, hyik hyik!" chuckled Sam, in a pathetic attempt to copy my magnificent villain's laugh. It takes years of practise to get it right, you know.

"No, Sam," I said wearily. "It's all in the back of the throat."

chapter 8

WE HAVE TO BE BRAVE AND FIND THE DIAMONDS

With Zebedee gone, who will save the world? Maybe Brian knows...

Zeebad sprang away, laughing his nasty laugh. Sam hurried after him. We struggled with the icicles blocking our way and eventually managed to push them aside. We dashed to the edge and peered into the crevasse. It went a long way down, and there was no sign of Zebedee.

There was a long, sad silence.

"We must leave now," said Ermintrude, eventually. "There's nothing more we can do here."

We walked back through the tunnel and to our camp. We packed up our stuff, boarded the train and resumed our journey. No-one said a word for a very, very long time.

"I can't believe he's really gone," sighed Ermintrude at last.

"Zeb's dead, baby," said Dylan. "Zeb's dead."

"Now who's going to help Florence and the children?" wailed Dougal.

"Cheer up, people!" I said, although I was just as miserable as the others. "We have to be brave and find the diamonds. After all, that was Zebedee's dying wish."

"Brian's right," said Dougal. "We're gonna save the world. Now where's the map?"

Dylan unfolded it, and we gathered round to study it.

"There!" I said, pointing. "Head for the highest mountain in that range."

"That's the spirit!" cried Dougal. "Nothing short of a sea of boiling lava will keep us from that diamond now!"

When we arrived, that's exactly what we found; a sea of boiling lava.

"Oh, sugar," said Dougal.

Ermintrude pointed to a pillar of rock which rose straight out of the lava.

"Well, that's where the diamond is. Who's going to get it?"

"Diamonds are a girl's best friend," said Dougal, shuffling backwards. "Off you trot, Ermintrude."

Ermintrude fixed him with a steely stare. "Men are supposed to give ladies diamonds. Not the other way around."

"I thought dogs were supposed to fetch things," said Dylan.

Dougal sat firmly down. "Well, my forte has always been 'sit'. That, and 'stay, Dougal. stay'."

"Surely it's only a short hop for a brave bunny," said Ermintrude, smiling sweetly at Dylan.

"More like a long drop for a dumb rabbit!" Dylan retorted.

I'd had enough. "QUIET!"

They looked at me, shocked.

"There's a bridge over there," I said.

The bridge was a narrow, crumbling causeway. It looked as though it might collapse at any moment. We climbed back into the train and edged gingerly onto the bridge. As it took our weight, fragments of the causeway broke off and dropped into the lava far below.

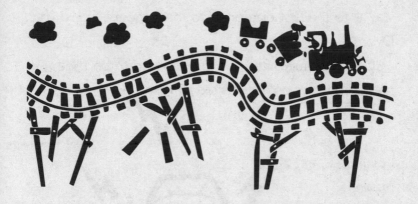

"Woah! Hot rocks, man," said Dylan, looking down.

Just as we passed the half–way point, one of the train's wheels slipped off the bridge. The train lurched to the side, scrabbling for a wheel-hold. Dylan worked the controls furiously.

"Dylan!" I yelled. "Do something!"

Dylan found the right button and pressed it. The train pulled itself back onto the bridge, and we chuffed at full speed across the rest of the causeway and onto the pillar. We breathed a big sigh of relief, and climbed out.

There in front of us, on a stone plinth, was a huge, glittering diamond.

"And there you have it!" announced Dougal. "I have led you all to the first diamond. Do the honours, would you, Dylan?"

Dylan carefully lifted the diamond from the plinth. As he put his paws on it, it started to hum.

I could see
moving
pictures in
one of the
diamond's faces.

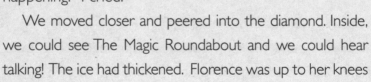

"Something's
happening!" I cried.

We moved closer and peered into the diamond. Inside, we could see The Magic Roundabout and we could hear talking! The ice had thickened. Florence was up to her knees in solid ice.

"I'm scared," Coral said.

"Come on, children," said Florence. "We have to be brave."

"It's Florence!" cried Dougal, excited.

Florence cocked her head slightly. "Strange," she said. "For a second there, I thought I heard... Oh, I must be going mad!"

Dougal turned a circle. "She can hear me!" he cried, then into the diamond:

"Florence! It's me! Dougal! I've come to save you!"

"Dougal?" said Florence, looking all around. "Is that you?"

The picture in the diamond started to fade.

"What's happening?" cried Dougal. "Nooooo!"

The picture disappeared.

"It's only been a day and they're freezing fast," said Dougal, fearfully.

A nose was blown violently right behind me. I turned to see who it was.

It was Zeebad! He blew his nose again and wiped his eyes. Tucking his hanky into his pocket, he recovered himself enough to speak.

"I'm not a monster, you know," he said. "I have feelings too. I mean, who could see all that beautiful ice and not be affected..."

He stopped. "What? You thought... Concerned for your friends? I don't think so! MWAAHA HA HA HAAAA!"

He moved forward, startling us. Dylan dropped the diamond.

"I'll take the map, too," said Zeebad, picking it up.

"Wait a minute," said Ermintrude. "How do you know there's a..."

Zeebad laughed, pointing at Dougal.

"They tortured it out of me!" Dougal cried.

"Give me the map," said Zeebad, springing forward again.

"Over my dead body," I said.

"Request granted!" said Zeebad. "Sam! Get out the garlic butter, I'm feeling a little peckish."

"You're bluffing," I said, but I wasn't so sure.

"Try me, you spineless slime-spreader," he said, staring me straight in the eye.

"Sticks and stones may break my bones, but names will never harm me," I said, my lips quivering.

"Very well," he laughed. "Bring out the sticks and stones instead, Sam!"

Ermintrude tossed the map to the ground. It landed at the base of Zeebad's spring.

"Here's the map," she said, sharply. "Leave him alone."

Dougal bristled.

"You're a despicable fiend," he growled.

"I know," said Zeebad. "It's a gift, really. Compassion is such a weakness."

He turned and bounced his way back over the bridge. Sam followed behind, copying his master's bouncing gait. The causeway quivered every time he landed. As Zeebad landed on solid ground, Sam landed with an extra-heavy thump. The causeway gave way beneath his feet and crumbled. Sam fell, but Zeebad stuck out a hand and grabbed him. "Good work, soldier," he said. "There's hope for you yet."

"Thank you, sir," said Sam.

Zeebad hauled him up, and they bounced away, leaving us stranded.

chapter 9

The gang need level heads now, and nobody's karma in a crisis than Dylan!

Man, what a bummer.
Stranded on a pillar of
rock in the middle of a sea
of boiling lava, and the
bridge is gone. Heavy.

"They don't make crumbling
rock causeways like they used to,"
I said. "Any chance it'll, like, grow
back?"

"At least we'll be nice and warm,"
said Dougal, miserably.

"Oh tragedy!" shrieked
Ermintrude, doing her drama
queen thing. "And just as I
was about to make it big!"

"You are big," said Dougal.

"Chill out, guys," I said. "I've
got something stashed that just might help."

"Dylan," said Brian, sighing. "We don't have time to
indulge in recreation..."

"Zebedee's magic box," I explained calmly, pulling the
gizmo out of my pocket.

There was one big red button on the box, and that was it. I stared at it for a moment or two.

"Now, if I could just get my head round how to work this thing," I said, scratching my head. "Did Zebedee give anyone the instructions?"

"JUST PRESS THE BUTTON!" they shouted at me. Like, okay!
So I did.

POOP!

The train's wagon turned into a boat. Pretty cool, but not exactly what I had in mind.

"A boat!" said Dougal, sarcastically. "Brilliant. It'll be plain sailing from here on in."
I had an idea.
"The tents!"

I got out all our tents and, like, sewed them together to make one giant sheet of canvas, then tied it to the train's funnel. It started to fill with hot air. Like, excellent! Soon, the train and the boat were hovering just off the ground.

"Come on, people," I said. "The sky's the limit now!"

We scrambled aboard and were soon floating high in the sky.

"A balloon escape," said Ermintrude. "You are clever, Dylan."

"It's all about altitude over attitude, Ermindude," I said.

"There is still one small problem," said Brian. "We have no idea where we're going."

Dougal panicked. Dougal always panics, man. "Brian's right. We could drift around for years!"

I pointed over the side of the boat. "Or we could, like, follow them."

Floating in a row boat on the sea beneath us were Zeebad and Soldier Sam. I let some air out of the balloon

and we dropped silently to hear what they had to say.

"Faster, Sam!" said Zeebad. "You row like a milkmaid."

"Ease up, sir," said Sam. "Now those pesky thieves are out of the way, what's the big rush?"

"Sam, imagine if you'd waited ten thousand years to come home to your frozen kingdom," said Zeebad, "Only to find a world covered in flowers! And animals! And sunshine! And— "

Sam clapped his hands. "Trees and rainbows and tiny little bunny rabbits and— "

"Shut up and row, you wooden windbag!" hissed Zeebad angrily. "Soon I will have the second diamond, and all those stranded simpletons will have is each other... for dinner!

Ha ha ha ha ha!"

Sam joined in, with an odd hiccupping laugh.

"Sam," said Zeebad. "You're ruining the moment."

"Sorry, sir," said Sam.

Totally uncool.

I let the balloon fill with hot air again, and we climbed back into the sky.

"We should get some sleep," I said, yawning.

"Is that all you ever think about?" asked Dougal.

"Sure," I said, drowsily. "Whenever I'm awake."

"I can't sleep," he said, but I wasn't listening too hard. "I'm too worried about my Florence. She's so helpless without me. She must be petrified."

"Pets? Fried?" I mumbled, half asleep. "Bad karma, man."

"Exactly," said Dougal. "I calm her down. The truth is I do everything for her. Her life would be quite empty without me there."

"Whoa," I said. "Don't toast the hamsters, dude!"

Maybe I wasn't paying too much attention to the hairy dog dude.

"During scary thunderstorms," he said. "She insists I climb into bed with her... for her protection. And she just loves to throw a tennis ball. Who's always there to bring it

back so she can have the pleasure of throwing it again? I'm telling you, Dylan, I bet she really misses that. Really, really misses that."

I think he might have sighed. Who knows, dudes? Who knows?

It seemed like it was only moments before Brian shook me awake. It was daylight already.

"Land ho!" he yelled.

He was right, too. Beneath us was a green island, all palm trees and bright flowers.

"Hey, man," I said. "Tropical vibes!"

I let some air out of the balloon and we dropped closer to the island.

Dougal kept watch up front. "Okay, everyone, prepare to land. Lower...lower..."

I let more air out of the balloon.

"Loads of room," said Dougal. "Lower... lower..."

CRASH! We smacked into the ground, and were thrown over the edge of the boat.

"Stop!" said Dougal.

He used us all as, like, a staircase to get to the ground.

"Perfect," he said.

Coming down is such a drag.

chapter 10

OH, FOR THE LOVE OF MOZART!

Ready for the next installment?
Heeeere's Ermintrude!

We picked ourselves up. Dougal was already eyeing up some enormous fruits which were dangling from a tree.

"Just in time for lunch," he said, stretching up to take the fruit in his mouth.

The fruit suddenly swung out of reach, and was replaced by a pair of giant snapping jaws! Dougal leapt backwards, narrowly avoiding the hungry plant.

"Looks like you're on the menu!" chuckled Dylan.

"I wonder where Zeebad is?" asked Brian.

"We must have overtaken him," said Dylan, patting the train. "Nice one, Train!"

"Wait here and keep your pistons pumping," said Dougal to the train. "We may need to make a quick getaway."

We made our way over to what looked like a temple. There were carvings all around the entrance.

"I wonder what these symbols mean?" I asked. They looked a little... fierce.

"Probably the ancient equivalent of a welcome mat," said Dougal, wandering past me through the doorway and into the passage beyond. I had my doubts. Bovine intuition, you know?

As he trod on a flagstone, it sank slightly. A spear whistled from a slot in one wall and slammed into the wall opposite, passing just above Dougal's head. He looked at the quivering spear for a moment, then backed out of the passage. The whole place was booby trapped!

"Where are my manners?" he said, shakily. "Ladies first."

I wasn't born yesterday, you know.

"No, after you," I said. "Age before beauty, dear."

"Oh, for heaven's sake, I'll go," said Brian.

I was stunned.

"Don't look so shell-shocked, Ermintrude," he said (I might have been staring). "I may be slow, but I can still take the lead."

He slithered into the passage at a gentle pace, leaving a slimy trail behind him.

"Ooh!" whispered Dougal. "Look who's beginning to grow a spine."

Brian made his way through the passage. As he went, he triggered every booby trap there was. Arrows, spears, rocks and snakes all appeared from the temple's walls, but he reached the end of the passage completely untouched.

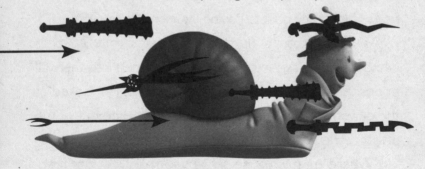

He turned and beckoned us to follow. "Come on, then. It's all clear."

But as he said those very words, a giant boulder crashed down from above. Brian disappeared.

We looked on, aghast. Then a dear little head popped round the boulder.

"Let's go," Brian said.

We hurried through the passage to catch up.

"What a snail!" I gasped.

At the end of the passage was a vast throne-room. Everything was covered in dust and cobwebs. It was very eerie.

"Anyone see the diamond?" called Dougal. His voice echoed around the chamber, making us all jump.

Dylan clutched at his heart. "Oh, Doog, man! Don't you know rabbits are kinda jumpy?"

Dougal climbed onto the dusty throne. "We must be in the wrong place," he said.

He saw a button on the arm of the throne, and pressed it.

"Cool! A recliner!"

There was an ominous rumble. From the floor rose a stone altar. On it, clutched in a stone claw, was...

"The second diamond!" cried Brian.

THUMP! THUMP! THUMP!

All the doors to the throne-room crashed down, trapping us inside. Laser beams appeared, criss-crossing every square metre of the room.

"Cool light show," said Dylan. He stretched out a paw towards one of the beams. "Hello, pretty lasers!"

"NOO!" yelled Brian. "They're alarm beams. If they're broken... well, I'm pretty sure something terrible will happen. Someone still has to get to the diamond, though."

Dougal popped a gobstopper into his mouth. "I'm too hairy."

Dylan lifted a trembling paw. "I've got the shakes."

I lost patience. "Oh for the love of Mozart! I'll do it. I trained as a ballerina, you know. My 'Swan Lake' was the talk of..."

"Stop milking the moment," said Brian, keeping perfectly still. His voice rose to scream: "AND GET ME OUT OF HERE!"

Some people have no class.

Using every last reserve of grace and agility (and that's a lot), I made my way towards the diamond. I squeezed, I twisted, I ducked, I leapt, I tip-toed. Finally, I stepped over the last beam. I had made it! I couldn't have been prouder if I'd brought the house down at La Scala.

"Ta—daaa!" I cried.

"Well done," cried Dougal. "That was brill..."

In his excitement, he forgot about the gobstopper in his mouth. It shot out, bounced once, twice, then rolled slowly across the floor, breaking one of the laser beams just before it came to rest.

"Oops!" said Dougal. Talk about an understatement.

The whole temple began to shake. From trap–doors in the floor, four ninja skeletons appeared. They surrounded us, ready for action.

I cleared my throat. "I don't suppose anyone knows anything about martial arts?"

chapter 11

Things are kicking off again, and Dougal's
thinking about his stomach. Typical!

"Just the basics of, like, kung-fu, kar-a-te, judo, kendo, tae-kwan-do, anything-you-can-do and tai-chi," said Dylan.

"Ooh!" I gasped. "Do those come with fried rice?"

"So, can you beat them up?" asked Brian, eagerly.

Dylan folded his arms. "Sorry, man. I don't believe in violence."

A ninja leapt into action, aiming a flying kick at Dylan's head. He caught the ninja's ankle and hurled him against the wall. The bones scattered.

"Except in self-defence," said Dylan, dusting himself down.

We cheered – until the bones began to slide together again. Bone by bone, the skeleton ninja was rebuilding himself!

"That's what I call pulling yourself together," said Dylan.

All four of the ninjas attacked Dylan. His
arm shot out and knocked one to
pieces. A lightning kick threw another
to the floor. He tossed one
over his shoulder and the
last got a
good
hard
thump on
the skull. A bony
arm rattled across
the floor to where I
was watching. I decided to
have a little lick (you can't look a gift bone in the mouth).

   As I licked it, the hand on the end reached up and
grabbed at me! I dropped the arm and retreated.

   Every time Dylan shattered one of the skeleton ninjas,
it reformed itself. The room was full of flying bones and
flailing fists as we battled for our lives. Ermintrude tapped
one ninja on the shoulder-bone with her hoof. When it
turned round, she smacked it, hard. The ninja collapsed.

   "I'm not just another pretty face," she said.

Dylan was in full martial arts overdrive and very impressive it was, too. He chopped, kicked, punched and threw until the skeleton ninjas were completely destroyed. Not one leg-bone was connected to a knee-bone or neck-bone connected to a shoulder-bone.

I stepped out from behind the pillar where I had been... er, waiting in ambush.

"Good group effort," I said. "Now let's get the diamond and head off."

I trotted towards the altar, but stopped in my tracks. The bones were moving again! They slid together and locked into place, forming one, gigantic skeleton monster!

"Uh-oh," I said.

"So!" boomed the monster. "The fearless warrior of legend has come to claim the diamond!"

"Er, no," I answered with barely a tremble in my voice. "The fearless warrior couldn't make it today, so we came instead. Er, we'll drop it in to him on the way home."

"Do you want the diamond or not?" asked the monster.

"If you're offering, yes," I said.

"I've got a better idea," yelled Brian. "Let's jump him! CHAAARGE!!!"

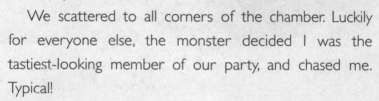

Brian slithered very, very slowly across the throne-room towards the skeleton monster, who laughed.

"Oh well," said Brian, giving up. "It was just a thought. Run away instead."

We scattered to all corners of the chamber. Luckily for everyone else, the monster decided I was the tastiest-looking member of our party, and chased me. Typical!

"Help!" I cried. "Dogs are supposed to eat bones, not the other way around!"

I jumped onto the throne again, and turned to find the monster almost upon me. In desperation, I hit another button.

The floor beneath the monster opened up and he dropped out of sight. I hit the button again and the floor closed over him.

"That was quick thinking, Dougal," said Ermintrude.

"Thanks," I said. "Anyway, enough chit-chat. Let's get the diamond and get out of here."

The diamond wasn't there.

"It's gone," said Brian, who likes to state the obvious.

"Zeebad!" I said. "He must have followed us!"

"Now he's got both diamonds!" wailed Ermintrude. "What are we going to do?"

"Don't panic," I said. "There's still one thing we've got over Zeebad – only we know where the final diamond is."

A familiar laugh rang out behind us. Sure enough, it was Zeebad and Sam. Zeebad held the second diamond.

"Looking for this, fools?" he sneered. "Now, tell me where the last diamond is!"

"No," I said, thinking of poor Florence.

"Resistance is futile," said Zeebad. "You're no match for the mighty Zeebad!"

"Pride comes before a fall," said Ermintrude. "NOW, DOUGAL!"

I hit the button again. The trap-door opened and Zeebad and Sam dropped out of the throne-room. I closed the trap-door over them.

"Hooray!" I cheered. "That's the last we'll see of them!"

"Yeah, man," said Dylan. "Except you just flushed away diamonds one and two."

"What now, then?" asked Brian.

"We must get back to The Roundabout as fast as we can," urged Ermintrude.

"I know there's, like, no rest for the wicked," said Dylan. "But I'm one of the good guys, and right now I need a siesta."

He leaned back against a sconce on the wall. It moved under his weight and a hidden door slid open. Through it was a secret passage!

We peered into the darkness, wondering what new horrors were in there. But it was a friendly noise that reached us!

"Toot-toot!"

"Typical train," I said. "Always turns up when you least expect it. Come on, gang. In we go."

We climbed into the train and started cautiously through the passage.

chapter 12

IT'S AGAINST MY NATURE TO SAY THIS, BUT... FASTER!

Time for a change of pace — here's Brian!

The passage was quite rough in places. The train lurched and bumped along.

"Oh, do slow down," cried Ermintrude. "You're making my milk churn!"

She's a very delicate cow, you know.

"Are you kidding?" said Dougal. "We're moving at a snail's pace!"

"Snail's pace suits me just fine," said Ermintrude.

I could have kissed her.

"That's the sweetest thing you've ever said," I told her. I may even have been blushed.

"Relax, Doogie," said Dylan. "This whole crazy trip will soon be behind us."

Dougal's hair stood on end. "Behind us!" he yelled.

"That's what I said, dude," said Dylan, yawning.

Dougal pointed over our heads.

"No – BEHIND US!" he shouted.

I turned to see what was upsetting him so much. If I had any hair, I'm sure it would have stood on end too. The giant skeleton monster was climbing aboard the carriage!

"It's against my nature to say this," I gulped. "But — Faster! Faster!"

The monster drew himself up, towering above us. I thought we were done for, but the monster hadn't noticed the beams holding up the roof of the passage. We sped beneath one and it caught him full on the forehead. The monster collapsed onto the track behind us, just a pile of old bones again.

"Woah, dudes!" said Dylan, wiping his forehead. "Talk about near-death experiences! I thought I saw the light at the end of the tunnel!"

"That IS the light at the end of the tunnel," said Dougal. "We're going to make it out of here!"

We shot out of the darkness of the passage and into bright sunlight. We were speeding across a bridge over a deep chasm.

"We're free! Zeebad's still trapped in the temple," said Dougal, grinning.

"Then, like, who's that?" said Dylan, pointing. "His evil brother, Zeebadder?"

Dylan was right. There was another bridge across the chasm. On it was a train (a much less friendly-looking one than ours) and on board were Zeebad and Sam.

The bridges swung towards one another, bringing Zeebad within earshot.

"Where's my third diamond?" he cried.

"Do something," shrieked Ermintrude.

Dylan scanned the train's control panel. He found a big button with a picture of a spring on it.

"An anti-spring device!" he said, excitedly. "That'll take care of Zeebad!"

"Are you sure?" I said, doubtfully. "Don't you think it might be..."

Dylan pressed the button, and I found myself soaring through the air.

"... AN EJECTOR SEEEEAAAATTTT!" I screamed.

I shot up and up. I looked back down. I could see the trains passing into a tunnel through a mountain. I looked straight ahead to see the mountain peak rushing towards me. I tucked my tail into my shell and cleared the peak by a millimetre. I stopped going up and started to fall. I thought I would be splattered on the tracks, but the trains emerged from the tunnel just in time. Suddenly, everything went black. I landed with a mighty thump.

"What the devil was that?" I heard someone cry. I still couldn't see a thing.

"Why am I blind?" I called. "Did we reach The Roundabout yet?"

"So that's where you're headed!"

Zeebad's voice sounded very pleased. And very close! I had landed on the wrong train!

"The Roundabout is where I'll find my diamond!" Zeebad cackled. "So long, slimeball!"

I rubbed my eyes and found that it was only my scarf which was blocking my vision. I pulled it out of the way and was faced with Zeebad and Sam.

"Get rid of the prisoner, Sam!" said Zeebad.

"I can't do that sir!" protested Sam. "Geneva Convention."

"Do it, Sam," was Zeebad's grim reply. "Guess what? I'm unconventional." I was starting to think he really had it in for me.

The evil one's train swooped downwards and, looking ahead, I could see its tracks would pass directly beneath the tracks of my friends' train. This would be my only chance to escape!

"Help!" I yelled.

Ermintrude nimbly lowered her tail over the side of their train. As Zeebad's train shot beneath, I reached up and took hold of the dangling tail delicately between my teeth. Before Sam or Zeebad could grab me, the clever cow lifted me straight back onto their train. What a journey, it's enough to put you off train travel for good!

chapter 13

IT'S NO USE CRYING OVER SPILT MILK

The chase is on — Ermintrude knows
they'll have to get a mooove on!

"Ermintrude," gasped Brian, panting on the floor of the train. "You saved me!"

I nursed my tail. He might have been a little more delicate with his teeth. After all, I did dramatically save his life. That's molluscs for you, I suppose.

"Uh-oh!" said Dougal. The two sets of tracks were converging again, and Zeebad was catching us! The engine of his train glowed red.

"Faster!" yelled Zeebad. "I want that diamond!"

Steam started to escape from the boiler of his train, and rivets began to pop out.

"The pressure's too much!" yelled Sam.

"I know," cackled Zeebad. "Sometimes I feel I'll go quite insane!"

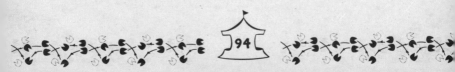

"No," said Sam. "The boiler..."

There was a huge explosion as the boiler cracked under the strain. Sam and Zeebad were launched into the air, and their train tumbled into the chasm beneath us.

"Thank goodness, we're safe," I said, breathing a huge sigh of relief.

I turned to look forward again, just in time to see the end of the line coming towards us at high speed.

We slammed into the buffers, and were pitched out of the train. Luckily, our landing was cushioned by the thick layer of snow on the ground.

Brian struggled to get his head clear of the snow. That's not easy when you have no hooves to dig with.

"We've got to get to The Roundabout before Zeebad," he said, trying to hurry everyone up.

"Zeebad doesn't know the diamond's there," said Dougal, shaking his tail free of snow.

Brian blushed. "Er, that's not strictly true... I ,er,... back on the train, I... er... might have let it slip."

"Oh, man," said Dylan. "This trip is getting worse!"

"Well, there's no use crying over spilt milk," I said.

"That's easy for you to say," muttered Dylan. I glared at him.

"Let's get back on the train and get there before him," said Dougal.

It didn't take long for us to see that the train wasn't an option any more. He'd obviously sprained a wheel, and was limping badly.

"Looks like this service has been cancelled," said Dylan.

"Poor trainy," I said.

"It's getting late," said Dougal. "The sun's already setting and we have to get there tomorrow. We'll just have to make it under our own steam."

Dougal was right. We were going to have to leave the train behind.

"Bye for now, old buddy," said Dylan.

"Just follow our tracks," said Brian. "You can make it!"

We started the long trek back to the village with heavy hearts.

chapter 14

WE'VE BEEN WALKING IN CIRCLES!

Things are getting hairy, so who better than Dougal to take up the story?

We struggled through the snow for what seemed an eternity. A blizzard had broken out, which made it really hard for us to see where we were going. We were completely exhausted.

"I can't go on," said Ermintrude, stopping. "We've been walking for hours."

"But if we don't get there soon, Florence and the children will be frozen stiff!" I said.

"It's so cold I can't feel my limb," shivered Brian.

I saw something in the snow. It was a trail of footprints!

"Footprints!" I cried. "Maybe they'll lead us back to the village."

Dylan examined the trail.

"These are, like, real freaky creatures! Look at the prints!" he said.

We all examined the tracks more closely.

"They're as exhausted as us," said Ermintrude. "One of them seems to be crawling along the ground."

Brian slid into the track she was talking about. His body filled it perfectly.

"I prefer the term 'gliding'," he said.

"Oh, no no no!" I cried, realising the awful truth. "We've been walking in circles!"

Dylan sat down, worn out and disconsolate.

"That's it, man," he said. "Time for the big sleep."

Ermintrude and Brian slumped to the ground as well.

"We did our best, and it wasn't good enough," said Brian, miserably.

"It's... it's the final curtain," mumbled Ermintrude, nodding off.

"No!" I shouted, "We mustn't sleep! It's too cold! We have to save Florence!"

But I was as tired as the others. My legs gave way and I lay down in the snow. In moments, I was fast asleep.

When I woke, I found myself in the most beautiful place I had ever seen. I stood on a path made of sugar-cubes. The trees were laden with barley sugars and fruity chews. Lollipops grew right out of the ground like flowers. In fact, everything was made of candy! It was... heaven!

Florence was standing right in front of me, beckoning me to her.

"Dooooougal!" she shouted. "Doooooougal!"

"Florence!" I said, happily. "You're ok!"

"I'm more than ok," she said. "I'm sweeeet!"

I was confused.

"But what about The Roundabout? The children? The snow?"

"Don't worry, Dougal," sang Florence, dreamily. "You're with me now..."

She vanished. Four little Florences appeared all around me, throwing me sweeties.

"...in sugar paradise!" they sang.

"Hmmm, sugar," I breathed, hardly able to believe my luck.

More Florences appeared. They tossed lollies and candy and boiled sweets and candyfloss. I was being showered with every sweetie known to man or dog.

The sweets piled up around me. As the pile got higher, it was harder and harder to keep my nose above candy. I began to panic. I was drowning in sweets! A thousand Florences were drowning me in candy!

"This can't be right," I said, struggling to throw off the weight of the candy. "Have to wake... wake up... save Florence. Florence!"

I woke up. The sun was just peering over the horizon. I was covered in snow. I shook it from my back, and set about waking the others.

"Wake up! Wake up!" I shouted.

"No way," said Dylan, turning over. "I'm in a higher state of unconsciousness."

"It's getting light and we're still completely lost," I said.

"Actually," said Brian. "I'm not so sure we are."

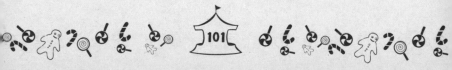

I looked around. As the sun rose, I could see more and more of our surroundings. I could hardly believe it – we had found the village!

"Woah," said Dylan, awake now. "That was some serious sleep-walking."

We walked into the village, trying to take in what had happened to it.

"This can't be our village," said Brian. "I don't recognise a thing."

"No, no, this is definitely it," I said, hurrying to the square. "If we go past this... white thingy... and round this... white bit, then just round this corner should be..."

We turned the corner into the village square and stopped.

"OH NO!" I cried.

We were too late.

chapter 15

Atten-SHUN! Stand up straight now —
here's Soldier Sam...

When the boiler exploded, Zeebad and I were shot into the air like fireworks. We rose up and up and up, and then fell down, down, down, landing painfully in the snow. I was knocked unconscious. When I came round, Zeebad was already up and about. I tried to get up, but every single bit of me seemed to be aching.

"Oooh, sir!" I cried. "Medic needed. SOS. May-day. Oooh!"

I didn't get the reaction I expected from my commanding officer.

"Me?" he sneered. "Help you? You treacherous mollusc-sparing disco dolly! Your tour of duty is over!"

He turned away.

"You can't leave an injured soldier, sir," I pleaded.

"Can't I?" said Zeebad. "Just watch me."

He bounced away.

"Wait!" I cried. "Come back!"

Zeebad's horrid cackling laugh faded into silence.

I laid my head back in the snow. Evil villains can be so cruel.

I must have passed out again because it was dark when I was woken by a strange sensation. I raised my head to see a blue moose, nudging me with his nose.

He seemed to want me to get up, so I struggled to my feet. There was no way I was fit for a long march so I hauled myself onto his back. The pain was terrible, but I kept thinking about what a fool I had been to do what Zeebad told me. I knew I somehow had to make up for the bad things he'd made me do, even it meant disobeying a superior officer. The moose and I set out for the village.

We got there just as dawn broke. Zeebad was on the roof of The Roundabout, obviously hunting for the third diamond.

"Curses!" he cried. "The diamond must be here somewhere."

"Zeebad!" I called.

Zeebad turned and stared at me as if I was a ghost.

"You!" he said.

I was cool and calm.

"This Roundabout ain't big enough for the both of us."

"When I leave someone for dead, I expect them to die," he said, springing down to the ground. "Can't you even do that right?"

"I haven't done anything right since I left The Roundabout," I said. "Now it's time for me to resume my post."

"You were on The Roundabout?" asked Zeebad, taken aback.

"I was guarding it from the likes of you," I said.

Zeebad laughed.

"Look at the state of you! You couldn't guard a boiled egg!"

I unsheathed my sword.

"My paintwork may have taken a battering, but it's like Zebedee told me. It's what's inside that counts."

I urged my moose into action and we charged at Zeebad. His moustache twinkled and a blast of that deadly energy struck the moose, freezing him solid. I was thrown from his back and landed heavily in the snow. Zeebad turned his moustache towards me and fired. He hit me on the chest, splitting me wide open. There, inside my body, twinkled the third diamond!

Zeebad bounced towards me, chuckling.

"Zebedee, you cunning swine," he said.

He plucked the diamond from my chest as I lay helpless.

"And to think I nearly abandoned it when I left you to die," he said, gazing at the jewel. "Oh, the irony!"

He turned back to face The Roundabout. I couldn't move a muscle to stop him.

"Now," cried Zeebad. "Time for the big chill!"

chapter 16

THIS GUY IS SERIOUSLY MESSING WITH MY KARMA!

It's high time for the return of Dylan!

The Roundabout was, like, totally frozen. On top of it was the bad springy dude, and he had all three diamonds. They hovered in the vortex above The Roundabout.

"I feel a cold front coming on!" I heard him shout. Crazy!

He put his shades on. Streams of ice shot from his moustache and hit the first diamond. Ice, like, fired out of the first diamond and into the second, then into the third. The stones glowed and hummed.

"ZEEBAD!" cried Ermintrude.

Zeebad turned and grinned.

"Perfect," he said. "You've arrived just in time for the finale."

He fired another blast from his moustache at the diamonds and a massive icy stream of pure energy, like, WHOOSHED into the air, hitting the sun. Ice started to grow on the sun. Freaky.

"We're doomed," said Brian. "Too late."

Dougal hurried to The Roundabout. He rubbed the ice with his nose and peered in.

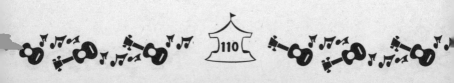

"This is all my fault," he wailed. "If only I hadn't been so greedy and stupid."

"Farewell, Dylan," said Ermintrude. "Goodbye, dear Brian."

Brian blushed. "Um, Ermintrude, before we freeze, there's something I've been trying to tell you..."

I wasn't listening to the snail. I hate it when dudes are bad to dudes, especially when they're bad to my dudes, you know?

"This guy is seriously messing with my karma," I said, gritting my teeth.

I picked up a handful of snow, packed it into a ball and threw it at Zeebad.

"Take this, you jumped up jack-in-the-box!" I shouted.

It hit Zeebad on the back of the head and knocked his sunglasses off. Good shot, dude!

"You don't know when you're beaten, do you?" he said, rubbing his head. "Take a chill pill, rabbit!"

He fired at me. I ducked and it hit Ermintrude on the tail. She squealed as hard as she could (and that's hard!). There was a loud cracking noise.

Dougal jumped back from The Roundabout as the ice splintered. Ermintrude's high note had damaged it!

"Sing, Ermintrude!" shouted Dougal. "Sing as loud as you can!"

"I'm not used to working under these conditions," she complained, dodging another blast from Zeebad. "And I haven't even warmed up."

"SING!" I shouted. Normally, you can't stop her singing!

She opened her mouth and sang. It was awful. Like, perfect.

Zeebad clapped his hands to his ears.

"What on earth is that abominable noise?" he cried.

More cracks appeared in the ice on The Roundabout. Ermintrude raised the pitch a little more and the cracks widened. As she hit the highest note she could, the ice on The Roundabout shattered, throwing Zeebad off his spring.

"Man, that is music to my ears," I shouted happily.

Zeebad growled.

I took hold of Brian's shell and lifted the little slimy dude onto Ermintrude's back.

"Shell loaded!" I cried.

Zeebad started blasting away again. I jumped out of the way. Ermintrude ran towards The Roundabout.

"Ready? Aim. Fire!" she cried, and flicked Brian into the air. Brian flipped onto the roof of a house on the square. He landed on his body and slid down the roof like he was snowboarding. He kicked off the edge and shot towards the diamonds.

"Wooah!" he yelled, knocking a diamond from its place in Zeebad's vortex.

"Yes!" I cheered. Way to snowboard, Brian!

Zeebad fired at me. I rolled out of the way and came to a stop right beside my guitar. Neal!

"Dylan! The diamond!" yelled Dougal. "It's coming your way!"

I grabbed my guitar.

"Cool," I said. "A sword for the stone!"

I swung the guitar at the flying diamond and whacked it, hard like a baseball bat. It landed in its slot on The Roundabout.

Brian landed back on the roof again and launched himself at The Roundabout. He flipped the last two diamonds towards Dougal.

"I got it! I got it!" said Dougal, excited.

Ermindude had other ideas. She barged him out of the way, which was a bit, like, rude, then hoofed the diamond into the second slot.

"Two-nil!" she celebrated.

"The game's not over yet," growled Zeebad.

Brian fell into his arms. They looked at one another, like, surprised, then Brian disappeared inside his shell.

The third diamond landed near Dougal.

"Touch it and you're dead," said Zeebad.

"You don't scare me!" said Dougal, standing over the diamond. "You're just a big blue bully. But now the tables have turned and all we have to do is put this last diamond back on..."

Zeebad threw Brian at the diamond. His shell knocked the diamond into the air.

I pulled my guitar back and waited for it to drop.

"Here comes a home run," I said.

Zeebad zapped my guitar from my hands, and knocked me over. He sprang towards the diamond and caught it.

"Ha ha!" he cried. "Victory!"

I shook my head. Man, what a bummer.

"So close and yet so..."

I saw something lying in the snow. It was Zebedee's magic box!

"Far out!" I said, and pointed the box at Zeebad.

I pressed the button... and nothing happened! I threw the box at him instead.

"Zebedee's toys can't help you now!" said Zeebad, laughing.

Something crashed into Zeebad from behind, knocking him down and tossing the diamond into the air again. It was one of our old friends!

"Train!" cried Dougal. "I knew you'd make it!"

"The diamond!" shrieked Ermintrude.

"I'll get it!" cried Dougal, running towards it. "I got us into this mess, and I'll get us out!"

He leapt into the air, evaded a blast from Zeebad and, like a footballer dude, headed the diamond into its slot. The ground began to shake, which was a bit, like, worrying, but then all the snow and ice was sucked into the whirling vortex above The Roundabout.

"NOOOO!" cried Zeebad, but the vortex was too strong for him. He was sucked in, too.

Cooool!

chapter 17

Every dog has his day, and it looks like
this one belongs to Dougal!

"Hurray!" cried Brian. "We did it!"

"Yeah, man, we did it," said Dylan.

"Of course we did it, darlings," said Ermintrude. "There's nothing like opera for breaking the ice. Ha ha!"

Dylan bent down and sniffed the ground.

"I can see grass, man! Sweet, green grass!"

I ran over to The Roundabout, the others following behind. Mr Rusty, Coral and Basil climbed off, shivering, but my Florence was still slumped on the floor.

"Florence? Can you hear me?" I said, with a lump in my throat. "Wake up. Don't leave me. This world means nothing without you."

Dylan put his arm on my shoulder.

"Sorry, old buddy," he said.

"It can't be true," I said, desperately.

"Florence. My lovely Florence."

I licked her gently on the face. Her eyelids fluttered.

"She moved!" cried Brian.

I licked her again and again, harder and harder. Florence started to come round.

"She's alive!" said Ermintrude.

I helped Florence to her feet and off The Roundabout.

"I thought I'd lost you forever, Florence," I said, hugging her.

"And I thought I'd lost you too, Dougal," she answered. "But you saved my life. And everyone else's."

I blushed.

"Oh, stop it. It's what any incredibly heroic dog would do."

"So you don't want a little... reward?" she smiled.

I shook my head.

"Oh no, I've learnt my lesson. I'm not having anything more to do with lollipops. Or gob-stoppers. Or lovely, lovely toffees..."

I think I might have been drooling.

"But wait!" exclaimed Florence. "Where's... what happened to..."

With a great SPROING, Zebedee landed in the square.

"Zipadi-dee, zipadi-da!" he said.

"Zebedee!" I cried.

"I always knew you could do it, my friends," he said.

"We thought you were dead," I said.

"Nonsense, Dougal," he laughed. "Everyone knows that after winter it's time for SPRING!"

He bounced into the air.

"Come on, then," said Florence, getting to her feet. "To The Roundabout!"

We jumped on board, but The Roundabout wouldn't turn, no matter what Mr Rusty did with the controls.

"How come it's not moving?" asked Brian.

"It's like, stuck, man," said Dylan.

"Don't you remember?" asked Zebedee. "The Roundabout's still missing something. Or should I say ... someone?"

Soldier Sam! We turned to look for him, but he was still lying on the ground where Zeebad had left him. The blue moose stood mournfully over him, nudging him with his nose.

"Sam?" I said. "But he was Zeebad's henchman!"

"Don't be too hard on him," said Zebedee. "He was a victim of Zeebad's magic too."

He took the third diamond from The Roundabout and placed it inside Sam's chest. One zap from Zebedee's moustache healed Sam's chest, and shrank him to his original size.

"It's time for you to go back where you belong, Sam," said Zebedee, and used his magic to lift Sam onto the canopy of The Roundabout, to resume his old position.

The music started and The Roundabout gently turned, in the right direction this time.

epilogue

The vortex opened and dumped Zeebad unceremoniously onto the ground amid a shower of ice and snow. He shook his head and got back to his spring. Stalagmites surrounded him on all sides.

"Curses!" he cried. "Imprisoned once more!"

He leant over to pick up some of the snow that lay on the ground.

"Ah well, at least it's cold."

The snow melted away in his hand. He looked at the floor of his prison. The ice and snow was melting there, too. Zeebad took hold of his prison bars and looked out. He

was perched on a rocky pinnacle in an underground cavern. Surrounding him on all sides was a sea of boiling hot lava. Zeebad began to sweat.

"Double curses!"

And so The Roundabout was back to normal. The friends had faced a terrible trial and made it through. Friendship and goodness won out over evil. The good times had returned. Zebedee watched as his friends resumed their happy lives.

Florence and Dougal were together again, Brian and Emintrude were getting along very well, and Dylan was fast asleep. The blue moose stood nearby, looking a little sad. Zebedee flexed his moustache and zapped him back to his original colour. The moose galloped off, much happier now.

Zebedee grinned.

"Everything worked out," he said. "In a *roundabout* kind of way!"

Zebedee

THE MAGIC™ ROUNDABOUT

There's more to this rabbit than meets the eye!

Gift Boxed Mugs

Light Activated Room Guard DYLAN™

Character Beanies

Press my tummy to hear me talk!

Talking FLORENCE™

ERMINTRUDE™ Back Pack

ViViD imaginations